STEEL FOR ALL

GALACTIC MERCENARIES

BOOK 3

OTHER BOOKS

Dragon Riders of Osnen

Trial by Sorcery
A Bond of Flame
The Warrior's Call
The Coin of Souls
Wing of Terror
Eyes of Stone
Tooth and Claw
The Servant of Souls
Smoke and Shadow
The Dark Rider
The Song of Bones
Sword and Crown
Tides of Darkness
Wrath and Ruin

Marked by the Dragon

Scale of the Dragon
Egg of the Dragon
Call of the Dragon
Wrath of the Dragon

The Fallen King Chronicles

Dragonsphere
The Fallen King
The Valiant King
The Restored King

STEEL FOR ALL

GALACTIC MERCENARIES

BOOK 3

RICHARD FIERCE

Cover design by 100Covers

Dragonfire Press

e-Book ISBN: 978-1-947329-22-5

Print ISBN: 978-1-958354-26-1

First Edition: 2023

1

JAYDE WAS SITTING IN Loch's customary seat on the *Determination,* waiting on the containment shield around Earth to be lowered. She felt odd piloting her own ship again. It had been a few years since Loch had joined her crew, and he had piloted the ship ever since. It wasn't like she didn't remember how to fly her own ship, it just felt … odd.

"What's taking so long?" Jayde demanded over the comms link.

"We're working on it," Loch's voice came back at her. "Are you sure Logan isn't really a doctor? I can barely read his handwriting."

"Just hurry up. I don't want to miss our window and have to try again tomorrow."

She stood up and walked to the window, gazing out at Earth. It was difficult to tell if the planet really was blue and white as she had seen on the holoscreen. The containment force field that surrounded the infected planet gave everything a lurid orange tint.

"I think we've got it," Loch's said. "Yeah, we got it. The shield is preparing to open."

Jayde hurried back to the console and sat down. She wasn't as quick on the screens as Loch was, but she didn't need to be quick. She just needed to be accurate. A long line grew across the shield, splitting it in half, and the two sides began to recede from one another.

"Logan didn't leave any other codes, did he?" Loch asked.

"No, why?"

"The shield won't open very much. I think it's going to be a tight fit."

It seemed nothing was ever easy, at least not for her and her crew. Jayde began tapping buttons on the console screen and the *Determination* moved forward slowly. As the vessel got closer to the opening in the shield, the ship's alarm blared loudly. Jayde flinched in surprise and saw a notification on the screen, alerting her that the right side of the ship was in danger of striking the shield.

"Loch, please remind me which button turns on the right-side thrusters?"

"It's the button that says 'Adjustment Right.'"

Of course. She remembered now that Loch said it. So, she was a little rusty. She wouldn't admit that to Loch, of course, but she was worried now that if she needed help, she might make a mistake. The shield affected communications from Earth, and if she couldn't get ahold of Loch, it could result in a disaster.

"Breathe," she whispered aloud. "I've got this."

Jayde pressed the adjustment button and the *Determination's* right side lowered until the alarm turned off. She surveyed the screen. Everything aligned correctly, and she increased the speed of the ship. The vessel passed through the opening with only a few feet to spare and Jayde exhaled the breath she didn't realize she'd been holding.

"We're through," she said.

"I see that," Loch replied. "Nice job."

The containment field was a few hundred feet above Earth's atmosphere. Jayde's eyes widened at the beauty of Earth. Wisps of clouds dotted the otherwise mostly blue landscape. From this distance, the spots of land looked like giant islands. Jayde had read that seventy-one percent of the planet was covered in water. No wonder the land looked like islands. She blinked a few times to clear the growing tears, then entered the coordinates Logan had given her into the ship's computer: 34.013071° N, -85.030200° W.

Jayde adjusted the trajectory of the vessel and watched as flames erupted around the ship as it entered the atmosphere. The *Determination's* shields held steady under the fiery temperatures and the ship burst free and plummeted quickly through the sky. Jayde tapped the screen and slowed the ship as it neared the ground. She spotted the open space Stefan had told her about and flew the ship toward the area.

Even when she had piloted the ship herself, landings had always been a problem. She tried her best not to worry about it, but she could feel the dread creeping into her stomach. The radar beeped as it picked up several forms moving in her direction. Thankful for the distraction, she focused in on the forms and quickly realized they were sleepers. She tapped the intercom.

"McCready, we've got incoming! I'd rather not land us in the middle of an army of sleepers."

"On it," the veteran soldier replied.

Jayde kept the ship in place and waited for McCready to man the plasma turrets. She was surprised when the cargo bay doors opened instead.

"What are you doing?" she asked.

"I'm taking the mech for a drive. It's a beautiful day, don't you think?"

Without another word, McCready leaped from the ship. Jayde quickly shut the bay doors and flew to the landing spot, worried more than before. She struggled with the controls and tried to land straight, but she wasn't sure what she was doing and the ship slammed down hard on the ground.

She turned the engines off and sprinted out of the observation deck to her personal quarters to grab her pistol. It was completely charged, but she knew it wouldn't be enough. Not even close. She grabbed a few cartridges and hurried to the elevator where she found Isa waiting. Four armed men, her personal guards, were with her.

"Do you need a weapon?" Jayde asked.

"No, thank you," Isa replied. "I've got my own." The young woman lifted a Silver Flux rifle and flashed a smile.

"Good. McCready's out there and he's surrounded by sleepers. We need to hurry."

The elevator doors opened and they filed in. Jayde's heart was pounding in her chest and in her ears. It felt like an eternity before the elevator stopped and she was able to run again. Isa and her guards exited the ship and Jayde closed the door, then ran as fast as she could to McCready's location.

There were a few small buildings blocking her view. One of them appeared to be a fueling station. Plumes of smoke rose from behind the building and Jayde pumped her legs harder. The ground sloped downward and she almost lost her footing but managed to keep from tumbling down the hill. Ahead, she could hear the grinding sound of the mech and McCready shouting. She lifted her pistol as she came around the fueling station.

McCready was surrounded by sleepers. The mech towered over them by several feet, but there was a sea of undead clawing at the machine. Jayde didn't know much about the war machines, but she assumed that if enough of the sleepers pushed on one side then the mech would tip over. She took aim and blasted one sleeper in the skull. The sleeper's head jerked roughly and brain and blood splattered those around it.

Jayde glanced over her shoulder and saw Isa and her guards fanning out wide. They began shooting and a wave of the sleepers went down. Jayde was upset when Isa had first boarded her ship. The girl had threatened to turn them in for the murder of her father, after all. Now? She was glad to have the girl and her guards. Jayde needed all the help she could get for this mission.

The mech swung its right arm and sent sleepers staggering backward. The other arm followed, but this one was armed with a laser gun. The laser blasts tore the sleepers to pieces and slowly the group of undead was cleared from the area. Jayde swapped cartridges on her pistol. The first one was down to ten percent charge. She quickly realized that she didn't have enough ammunition to make it to the survivor's camp and back.

"We've got to go back to the ship," Jayde said. "We're going to need more guns."

Isa motioned for her guards to stay put and she walked over to Jayde.

"I'll go with you," she said. "They can stay here and keep watch with your guy."

"His name's McCready," Jayde said.

"Right, sorry. I keep forgetting his name."

"Don't worry about it," Jayde said. "Let's go. I'm sure all that noise is going to draw every sleeper for miles. The quicker we can get the survivors out of here, the better."

"I don't disagree," Isa said.

They trudged back up the hill toward the ship. It wasn't long before Jayde's leg muscles started hurting from the exertion. She hunched forward and gritted her teeth against the burning sensation. Jayde was forced to stop about halfway to take a break. Isa also stopped, but she didn't seem fazed. Hell, she wasn't even breathing heavily. That left Jayde to ponder if she was really that out of shape.

"Why did you come down here to help?" Jayde asked, suddenly curious.

Isa looked at her. "I have my reasons."

"I figured as much. Mind sharing them?"

"Not really," Isa replied.

Jayde shrugged. She assumed it had something to do with Loch. Maybe the girl felt like she needed to prove herself somehow? Jayde could only guess. The burning in her legs had subsided enough that she felt she could continue the climb. She marched the rest of the way and didn't stop until they reached the top of the hill. Jayde paused only long enough to rub her thighs, then continued to the ship.

The armory had an assortment of weapons, most of them McCready's. Jayde selected a rifle similar to Isa's Silver Flux, grabbed a belt with plasma grenades, and filled a bag with cartridges for the rifle and her pistol. Isa filled two bags and they left the ship again. Jayde hoped what they carried was enough.

As they reached the hill, Jayde stopped and looked around at the landscape. The entire area looked like a warzone. She wondered how beautiful it must have been before the Thraan attacked.

"What is it?" Isa asked. She blocked the sun from her eyes and peered down the hill.

"Nothing," Jayde said. "Let's go."

Jayde's legs felt like jelly as she descended the hill. Her muscles complained with every step, but she ignored the pain and focused on the task at hand. She wanted to get the survivors to the *Titan* before sundown. Earth was beautiful, but she knew all too well that the most beautiful things held the most danger.

She was tempted to stop and rest again, but time was against them. Jayde did find small comfort in the fact that she was outpacing Isa by about ten feet. She glanced back at the woman. Isa looked like she was struggling under the weight of the bags she was carrying. Jayde smirked. Her legs might be screaming in agony, but her arms were holding up much better than Isa's.

"Need some help?" she called out.

"No," Isa huffed, cheeks flushed.

Jayde was about to say something else, but she noticed a circular spot on the ground in front of Isa that looked … different. Jayde stopped and raised a hand in warning, but Isa wasn't looking at her.

"Stop!" Jayde shouted.

It was too late. Isa looked up as she stepped on the circle and the ground caved in beneath Isa's foot. She disappeared into a large hole with a surprised cry, then a moment later the cry turned to a blood-curdling scream. Jayde rushed to the edge of the hole and looked down. It was about six feet in depth. Isa was in a sitting position, a long wooden stake protruding from her thigh. Blood was everywhere.

Jayde looked back toward McCready and the guards. Two of the men were running in her direction. She waved at them, urging them to hurry.

"Hold on, Isa! We're going to get you out of there!" Jayde screamed.

Jayde tossed her bags down and set the rifle on the ground beside them, then looked back in the hole. There were a few other wooden stakes in the hole, but Jayde figured she could climb down safely without impaling herself. She looked at the guards again. Their pace had slowed, but they were still coming. There was something else, too.

Sleepers.

At least a hundred of them were approaching the fueling station. The guards weren't going to reach her in time to help. It was up to her. It was *always* up to her. Jayde groaned and climbed down into the hole.

2

THE WOUND LOOKED WORSE up-close.

Jayde knew immediately that Isa was going to lose the leg. The wooden spike was roughly six inches in diameter, which left little flesh keeping the leg attached. Isa's screams weren't helping anything, and Jayde was seriously considering punching the woman into unconsciousness when Isa's eyes rolled into her head and she passed out.

"That'll make part of this easier," Jayde muttered.

She could hear gunfire and knew the sleepers had reached McCready and the others. Jayde stared at Isa's mangled leg and considered how to free her from the wooden pole. This wasn't the ideal place to cut her leg off, nor was she a doctor anyway. Maybe she could pull the pole the rest of the way through the wound?

Her decision was made. Jayde wrapped her hands around the wooden pole and tried to heave it up. It didn't budge, but she didn't know if that was because it was too heavy or because it was attached to the ground. A quick survey of the pit floor revealed that the spike was connected to something under the dirt.

Jayde grabbed ahold of the pole again and twisted it counter-clockwise. She grunted from the exertion and pushed as hard as she could. Just as her strength was about to fail, the pole twisted an inch. Spurred by the small victory, Jayde twisted the pole again. This time, it was easier and it turned a full circle. She continued twisting the pole around and around until it came loose, then she squatted low and used her legs to heft the pole up.

The weight and height of the thing almost sent her sprawling, but she managed to catch her balance and used the pole's momentum to hurl it to the other side of the pit. The amount of blood gushing from Isa's wound made Jayde's stomach drop. There was so much of the red liquid that it was pooling under Isa's still form.

"We need medical supplies!" Jayde screamed as loudly as she could.

She didn't know why she bothered. The others were occupied with fending off the sleepers, but she felt helpless down here. Jayde checked the walls of the pit for a ladder or some way out. There was nothing.

"I can do this," she muttered, glancing around the pit again. It was obvious she wasn't going to be able to carry Isa out of the pit. She would have to get herself out and then find something to pull Isa up with.

Jayde grabbed onto one of the poles and placed one foot on the wall of the pit, then shuffled upward, alternating between her leg and arm strength. She slid down a few times, getting frustrated with herself and stressing over the knowledge that Isa was bleeding out. Finally, after much cursing and a few tears, she climbed out of the pit.

The two guards who had tried to run to Isa's aide were dead, their bodies nothing more than mangled messes. McCready's mech was still blasting sleepers to pieces and the two remaining guards were backed against a dilapidated building. She looked down into the pit. Isa was still unconscious, but it appeared her bleeding had stopped. It was hard to tell, though.

"Rope," Jayde said. "I need a rope."

She considered running back to the ship to get some, but it would take too long. Isa would be dead before she got back. Jayde noticed a pile of debris nearby and rummaged through it, looking for anything that might serve as a rope. She found a long aluminum wire that looked like it might have once been attached to the steel poles that littered the area, possibly a fence. It was more than long enough and she wrapped it around her waist and ran back to the pit.

Jayde noticed the gunfire had ceased, but she didn't see the guards or the mech. She couldn't worry about that. She debated on tossing the wire down but instead decided to keep it around herself and carry Isa up. The wire was long enough, and when she jerked the line, it didn't budge much farther than its current length. Satisfied, Jayde repelled down into the pit. Isa was groaning, but her eyes were closed.

"Hang in there," Jayde said. "I'm getting you out of here. Just hang on."

Isa was lighter than she looked, and Jayde had little trouble slinging the woman over her shoulder. She did her best to keep Isa's wound from hitting anything on the way up, but as she reached the top of the pit and dropped Isa onto her back, the woman became conscious and started screaming in pain again.

"You've got to keep quiet! They're going to hear you, Isa!"

"I can't," Isa moaned. "It hurts so bad!"

"I know it does. I'm going to take of care of you, but you've got to be quiet or neither one of us is going to make it."

Too late, Jayde realized as she spotted more sleepers coming up the hill toward them. There was still no sign of McCready or Isa's guards. Had they all been killed? No. Jayde wouldn't entertain that fear. If McCready died, she was screwed.

"We need to get back to the ship," Jayde said. "Do you think you can walk with my help?"

Isa looked down at her leg and grimaced, then shook her head. "I don't think so," she answered. "I can't feel anything."

Jayde hoped Isa meant that she couldn't feel anything in her leg. If she couldn't feel *anything,* then it was already too late for the woman. She grabbed ahold of Isa's arm and tried to pull the woman to her feet. Despite Isa being lightweight, it was a major struggle.

"This was easier when you were unconscious," Jayde said.

"I'll keep that in mind when I feel like I'm going to pass out," Isa said sarcastically.

That brought a grin to Jayde's lips and she had to admit that Isa was a tough one. Her leg was barely hanging on and she could still manage some humor. Jayde's respect for Isa continued to grow.

The sleepers were slowly making progress up the hill. Jayde gave up trying to get Isa onto her feet and opened one of the bags she'd brought from the ship and pulled out a plasma grenade. Jayde pressed the button and tossed it down the hill. A few seconds later, a concussive explosion rocked the ground. Jayde confirmed the closest sleepers had been blown to bits and looked down at Isa.

"I can get to the ship and back with stuff for your wound before we'll reach it together."

There was a fear in Isa's eyes that Jayde had seen many times in other people. It was the fear of dying.

"I won't leave you if you don't want me to, but there's a good chance you'll die from blood loss."

Tears rolled down Isa's cheeks but she nodded stiffly. "Go. Please hurry."

Jayde sprinted back to the *Determination*. She didn't allow anything to cloud her thoughts. The only thing she allowed herself to think about was getting Isa patched up and onto the ship. Nothing else mattered at this moment. Jayde boarded the vessel and headed for the infirmary, grabbing gauze and antiseptics in a crazed frenzy.

She rushed back to Isa and saw McCready's mech nearby. The soldier was kneeling beside Isa and Jayde felt a weight lift off her shoulders. McCready was alive.

"She's going to be fine," Jayde huffed as she dropped to her knees beside Isa. "Oh great, she's passed out again."

"No," McCready said. "She's dead."

"Isa's not dead," Jayde argued. "She's just lost a lot of blood. I'll cover the wound and she'll be fine."

"Jayde." McCready grabbed her hand. "Look at her."

Jayde looked at Isa's face. The woman's skin was relaxed and her eyes were closed, but otherwise, she looked fine. Jayde started to shake her head, but then she noticed how pale Isa was. She stared at Isa's neck for a pulse but there was no movement, so she placed two fingers on the woman's flesh and confirmed her fears.

Isa *was* dead.

"Her guards?" Jayde asked without looking up.

"Dead," McCready grunted. "It's just me and you."

Jayde digested the information. It didn't seem real; it couldn't be real. They had just landed. How could five people be dead within minutes of landing? She met McCready's eyes.

"I don't think I can do this," she whispered.

"You have to," McCready replied. "Stefan and those with him are waiting for us."

Jayde knew he was right. She couldn't give up. It was her idea to come down here and play rescuer. What kind of person would she be if she let Isa's death be for nothing? If she left innocent people stranded, surrounded by sleepers?

"I'm glad you're here," Jayde said.

"I'm not," McCready smiled. "Let's get moving before more dredges show up."

McCready climbed back into the mech and Jayde strapped the bags Isa had brought onto the back of the machine, then grabbed her rifle and her own bags. They headed down the hill and Jayde saw the other two guards had died where she'd last seen them, trapped with their backs against the building.

The ship's navigation showed the location of the Remnant being roughly half a mile away. Once they reached the bottom of the hill, the landscape remained flat and easy to cross. They passed burned-out buildings, corpses of sleepers and their victims, and the remains of small bastions of defense. The people here had really put up a fight, but in the end, it hadn't stopped the undead.

They encountered several small groups of sleepers on their way and always stopped to blast them to hell. The fewer sleepers they ran into on the way back, the quicker they would be able to reach the *Determination* and get off the planet. Jayde checked the distance on her holoscreen and saw they were getting close.

"Not much farther!" She had to yell for McCready to hear her over the sound of the mech. He gave her a thumbs up. Jayde kept the holoscreen up and zoomed in on the map. As they turned down a street riddled with holes from laser blasters, there was a commotion ahead. Jayde could make out figures running and the sound of gunfire echoed off the buildings.

Jayde picked up the pace and ran toward the figures. As she got closer, she saw it was two women. One of them was hurling rocks at an approaching sleeper and the other was holding up a pistol. The woman was pulling the trigger, but the cartridge was dead and the gun merely made a clicking sound. Jayde grabbed a spare cartridge from her bag and tossed it to the woman, who missed catching it. The cartridge fell on the ground, but Jayde brought her rifle up and scored a headshot on the sleeper.

"You must be Jayde Thrin," the woman throwing rocks said. "I'm glad to see you!"

"That's me," Jayde said. "What's happening?"

"We were ambushed by the dredges. They figured out our routine and were waiting on us."

Jayde's face scrunched in confusion. "They what? How did they do that? They're mindless."

The woman gave Jayde a look but didn't explain.

"Where's everyone else?" Jayde asked.

"Down there," the woman pointed toward the end of the street. "Stefan and the others were traveling closer together and they got trapped at the blockade."

Jayde took off in the direction the woman pointed, not waiting to see if McCready was following. She came across a few sleepers straggling behind the main group and blasted their heads open with her rifle. At the sound of gunfire, some of the other sleepers broke away from the group and came toward her. These sleepers looked different from the ones she'd encountered on M44. They were less dead looking and almost seemed aware.

She blasted her way through them and continued to the blockade. A few of the survivors were behind the blockade, shooting and throwing rocks at the sleepers that had them surrounded. Jayde was about to come to their aid when she saw a young girl surrounded by the undead. They were quickly closing in on her.

Jayde lifted her gun and took aim. It was the only child in the group, and she wasn't going to let the sleepers kill Stefan's daughter.

3

JAYDE CHECKED THE CARTRIDGE charge level. It was depleted. She dropped the bags she carried and sprinted toward the girl, swinging the rifle like a club and smashing the heads of sleepers with the butt end of the gun. The girl had her hands over her ears and was huddled down on the ground. Jayde stood in front of the girl and drew her pistol.

A familiar voice was shouting orders to people. Jayde looked to her left and saw a rugged, dirty man pointing to a group of sleepers trying to climb over the blockade. He lifted a homemade spear and flung it at one of the sleepers, striking it in the chest. It reeled backward and fell to the ground. The man wore a rifle over his shoulder, but he grabbed anything around him that could be used as a weapon, slashing and stabbing sleepers, knocking them in the head with rocks. The man was like a beast. A sleeper was on the ground, crawling toward him from behind. Jayde took aim with her pistol and fired, blasting the undead's brains from its skull.

The man, whom Jayde believed to be Stefan, looked at her in surprise. He waved and continued directing his people in the defense of the blockade. Jayde looked for McCready, but she didn't see the mech anywhere. The crowd of sleepers was growing exponentially. Stefan and the other survivors were holding them off, but Jayde didn't see that lasting much longer. She looked around for a better place to defend.

A square, short building with boards covering the doorway was the closest option. Jayde grabbed the girl's hand and pulled her to her feet, then dragged her to the boarded doorway. Jayde kicked at the wooden planks, trying to break them in half. Some of them were too thick to break, but a few yielded to her force and snapped in the center. She used her pistol to blast other boards free and pushed the girl inside.

"Stay in here," Jayde shouted. "Find somewhere to hide!"

Jayde turned and ran to where she had dropped her bags and retrieved them both. She looked around again for McCready and found him helping Stefan. The two were standing shoulder to shoulder, blasting sleepers left and right.

"Inside the building!" Jayde shouted.

A few of the survivors glanced at her. She motioned to the building. "Hurry!"

The survivors looked to Stefan for approval. He looked at them, then to the building. Jayde saw McCready say something to the man, but she couldn't hear what he said. Stefan looked at the swelling ranks of sleepers and shouted, "Fall back! Get inside the building!"

Jayde stood beside the door and offered cover for those running inside. She shot off a few blasts, picking off a couple of sleepers that were getting too close. The last few survivors made it into the building safely, followed by Stefan and McCready. Jayde shot two more sleepers and then ducked inside.

"We need to block the doorway!" She shouted.

McCready and Stefan pushed a tall metal cabinet in front of the door. It blocked most of the doorway, but Jayde didn't think it would keep the sleepers at bay for long.

"That's not going to be enough," she said. "Let's move that desk over here, too."

The three of them heaved the desk across the room and pushed it in front of the cabinet. It was sturdy and heavy, and Jayde hoped it was enough to keep the cabinet from budging. She surveyed the room and saw it was made up of several small office spaces. There was another door leading outside, but it was closed and deadbolted.

"We can rest here for a few minutes. Once the sleepers lose interest, we'll get moving. How many of you are left?" Jayde asked.

Stefan rolled his neck, reminding her of McCready. The two men didn't look anything alike, but they had many of the same mannerisms. She guessed Stefan must have been in the military as well.

"We only lost one," he said, lowering his voice. "He was an elderly man and couldn't outrun the sleepers, but he yelled a warning as he went down.

His death alerted us to the dredge ambush, or we'd have lost many more."

"I don't understand," Jayde said. "The sleepers, dredges, whatever, can't think. They don't have the ability to make plans and ambush people."

Stefan looked at her as if she was crazy. "Says who?"

Jayde looked at McCready for support.

"I served with the Convocation is deep space," McCready said. "I've never seen a dredge that could use its brain."

"We encountered some on a mining planet a few weeks ago. They're not capable of thinking." Jayde was worried that these people might have lost their sanity from the heartbreak of watching their friends and loved ones die so horribly.

"I can't say what you've seen or haven't seen," Stefan said, "but I can tell you what we've seen. Those things aren't mindless creatures. They're intelligent and cunning. Whatever you've come across before is nothing like these dredges."

Stefan was too confident with his words for Jayde to believe the man had lost his wits, but the idea that sleepers could plan an ambush was hard to wrap her mind around. Jayde looked around the room at the other survivors. They were all in a disheveled state. Dirty, torn clothing, frightened. Stefan's daughter was standing beside a woman who held the girl's hand protectively.

"Is that your wife?" Jayde asked with a nod of her head. Stefan shook his head.

"No. That's Janice. She lost her daughter in the attack and has taken Anna under her motherly wing. She'd been a lifesaver more times than I can count."

"What happened?" Jayde asked. "When the Thraan attacked, what happened down here?"

Stefan's expression grew dark. "Logan's dead, isn't he?"

"What? No, he's alive." Jayde blinked in confusion.

"He knew about everything that happened. If he's not dead, why don't you know the details? Why does your rescue team only consist of two people?"

Jayde wasn't sure if she should tell him the truth. Considering they would probably never see Logan anyway, she guessed it ultimately didn't matter.

"The Convocation ordered him and the entire crew from the *Titan* to the front lines. The Thraan are threatening to invade human colonies."

"What about us?" Stefan asked.

"Logan was told that Earth was a lost cause. He wanted to help; he really did, but … his hands were tied. He left the code to the containment shield with me and I decided to do what I could. Two of my men on the *Titan* right now. There were others with us when we landed, but they were killed on the way here."

"I'm sorry for your loss," Stefan said. "We're out of food, which is why we left the safety of our base in the first place. It's a good thing you arrived when you did, or we might have been overrun."

"I don't think we're in the clear yet, especially if what you say about the sleepers in true. They could be trying to find a way inside now." Jayde opened one of her bags and transferred the pistol cartridges to the other bag, then handed Stefan the first bag. It contained some rations, and Stefan distributed the food among the survivors.

"Where are the other bags?" Jayde asked McCready.

"They're still on the mech," he said. "I didn't have time to grab them."

"We've got more guns, but they're with the mech," Jayde told Stefan when he rejoined them. He was chewing granola and brushed some crumbs from his beard.

"It's too dangerous to go back there," he said. "I'd love to have more guns, but it's not worth the risk."

Jayde didn't completely agree, but she also didn't feel like arguing. Her entire body ached and she wanted to lie down somewhere and sleep for days. As much as she wanted to rest longer, she knew they needed to hurry back to the *Determination.*

"Did you land at the coordinates I gave you?" Stefan asked.

"Yes." Jayde set her bag down and leaned against the wall for leverage as she slid down to the floor and crossed her legs. It felt good to be off her feet.

"Good. We should be able to get to your ship quickly, assuming the dredges don't have anything up their sleeves. You asked what happened here. I'll tell you if you really want to know, but it's not pretty."

"You ever heard what happened on Ochillon?" Jayde asked.

"Bits and pieces," Stefan said, finishing off his granola.

"I was there when it happened," Jayde said.

Stefan stared at her intently for a long moment before speaking.

"What happened here makes Ochillon look like a cake walk. We had no warning. It was a normal day and I was working in my shop as usual. There was a loud boom, like an explosion, but it was everywhere at once. I walked outside and the entire sky was red like blood. I had no idea what was happening. A lot of people came outside to stare at the sky. We didn't know any better.

"The redness in the sky was the disease the Thraan dropped into our atmosphere. These little red particles that looked like strings came floating down, covering everything as snow does. They reminded me of party streamers. People held their hands out and caught them. That was our first mistake. The disease moved quickly, turning people into dredges within moments of touching the stuff. Anna had come outside and I was going to take her into the house when I saw my wife standing there with a handful of red strings.

"The look in her eyes shook me so badly that I almost didn't react in time. She attacked me and tried to kill Anna."

Stefan stared off into the distance, reliving the memory. Jayde looked down at the floor and remained quiet. It was similar, yet so different, from what she'd experienced on Ochillon. The Thraan must have made tremendous leaps with the disease for it to react within minutes. It had taken hours on Ochillon before anyone knew something was wrong.

"I tried to talk some sense into her," Stefan continued. "She was growling and clawing at me, but I held her back and kept Anna safe. My wife wouldn't stop, though. She tried to bite me and I grabbed her by the jaw. I was just going to hold her in place until she came to her senses, but I noticed other people doing the same thing. They attacked their family members. People began screaming.

"Some of the screams were cries for help as they bled to death in the street. It slowly dawned on me that whatever those red strings were, they were responsible for the change. I told Anna to get into the house and then I did the hardest thing I've ever done in my life.

"I killed my wife. Looking back, she was probably already dead from the disease, but I snapped her neck and pushed her to the ground like a piece of trash."

Jayde could see tears in Stefan's eyes. She hated that anyone had to know the pain she did. The pain of killing a loved one that had turned into one of those horrific creatures. Stefan cleared his throat and wiped his eyes with his knuckles.

"Everything else is a blur," he said. "I think some of us were immune to the disease because we didn't turn even if we touched those string things. Anna and I moved from building to building, looking for food and other survivors. Our group grew quickly, but there were a lot of people who decided to go off on their own. Most of them are dead now. I've seen their corpses."

Jayde didn't know what to say. She'd been through it herself, but nothing anyone said to her ever helped. Stefan was nursing his left arm and she saw that he'd been bitten. The wound was infected but she didn't have the chance to say anything as the desk and cabinet screeched across the floor and sleepers flooded into the building.

4

Jayde scrambled to her feet and started blasting sleepers with her pistol.

She quickly swapped cartridges and picked up her bag, slinging it over her shoulder. The undead streamed through the doorway with no end. A huge crowd stood outside the building, all of them pushing to get in.

"Everyone out!" Stefan shouted. "Through the back! Go, go, go!"

McCready strapped his Silver Flux rifle over his shoulder and pulled two pistols from his waistband and started shooting. Jayde and the soldier blocked the escaping survivors with their bodies and laid waste to the sleepers that flooded into the building.

She fired as quickly as her fingers would pull the trigger, but it wasn't fast enough. There was too many undead. She swapped cartridges twice before McCready shouted that they needed to go. They walked back toward the exit, killing more sleepers before they crossed the threshold. Jayde reached into her bag and pulled out a plasma grenade, pressed the button, and tossed it into the building. It rolled over the debris and stopped next to a support beam. Jayde and McCready were sprinting down the street when it exploded and demolished the entire building.

They turned left and ended up back on the street they had come down when they ran into Stefan. He and the other survivors had regrouped not far from the blockade. Jayde could see more sleepers coming from all directions.

"This is bad," she huffed, looking at McCready.

"I don't disagree," he grunted. "We need to get back to the ship, but the dredges are everywhere."

"We need a diversion. Something to draw them away from the direction we need to go. Any ideas?"

McCready scratched his chin in thought, then shrugged his large shoulders. "I could take the mech and draw them somewhere long enough for you to get them out of here?"

Jayde considered the option, but she wasn't sure if splitting up was the best option. She looked at Stefan. He was kneeling in front of Anna and talking to her. The girl was crying. Jayde's curiosity was piqued.

"What's going on over there?" she asked McCready. The soldier grunted in reply. A moment later, Stefan hurried over to them.

"I need to ask you something. The dredges are coming in full force, and we don't have much time. Promise me you'll take care of my daughter."

"I'm sorry?" Jayde asked. "What are you talking about?"

"I know you saw my wound," he replied, lifting his arm to show the grisly sight. "I'm infected and I can feel the disease inside me. I've been burning up since the dredge bit me. I don't want my daughter to see me turn. It's bad enough she lost her mother the way she did. Please, Jayde? Please do this for me."

There were a hundred reasons or more that Jayde wanted to give Stefan as to why she couldn't make that promise. Their mercenary lifestyle was no place for a child. And that was assuming they even survived getting off Earth. Instead of saying anything, she merely offered a mute nod.

"Thank you," Stefan said, his relief evident.

"Where are you going?" Jayde asked him.

"As soon as you start leading the others to your ship, I'm going to do my part here."

His cryptic answer didn't tell Jayde anything, but she was too exhausted to question him further. McCready shook hands with Stefan and then headed for the mech. Jayde stood silently, watching the sleepers slowly closing in. She was starting to have serious doubts that any of them would get off the planet.

Jayde joined McCready by the mech and retrieved the bags of weapons and ammunition from the machine, then began handing them out to the survivors. There weren't enough guns to go around, so the people began grabbing things from the debris that they could use to defend themselves with. The sleepers were getting too close for Jayde's comfort.

"We need to go," she said loud enough for everyone to hear.

"Take care of Anna," Stefan said.

"I will," Jayde replied. She looked around for the girl and saw she was holding hands with Janice.

"Go," Stefan said. "I don't want Anna to see."

Jayde nodded and turned away from him. She had her suspicions of what he intended to do, and she agreed with him. Anna didn't need to see her father die.

"Guns up and ready!" Jayde shouted.

Behind her, the motorized grumbling of the mech reverberated in the air. The survivors who were armed with the guns she provided took the lead. Jayde jogged to join them. She quickly checked her cartridge level and rolled her shoulders. Her body was begging for rest, but she ignored the protests of her muscles. There would be time for rest when she was dead.

Jayde stayed in front of the group by a few paces, pistol up in front of her. She continuously looked left and right, keeping watch as the sleepers on the other streets began to close in. The ground vibrated under her feet with every step the mech took.

"Look out!" Someone shouted.

Three sleepers had crossed onto the street beside the survivors that didn't have guns. Those that did opened fire, taking the sleepers down quickly.

"We've got to pick up the pace!" Jayde yelled.

She started walking faster and led the group along the street, backtracking the steps she and McCready had taken to reach the survivors. The area looked the same, but there was something that felt off. Jayde knew better than to ignore her instincts.

"Keep your eyes open. I've got a bad feeling we're about to—"

Before she could finish her sentence, a mob of sleepers poured into the street ahead of them. There were dozens of them. Others staggered out of empty buildings, filling their ranks. Jayde wasted no time and started blasting them with her pistol.

"Take them down!" She screamed.

The group of men and women behind her started shooting into the crowd of sleepers. More and more continued to fill the street and Jayde was starting to get nervous.

"Get down!" It was McCready. Jayde dropped to the ground and covered her head. The mech's gun roared to life and laser blasts filled the air above her, cutting down masses of sleepers. Despite the power of the mech's weapons, the ranks of the sleepers were still growing. It looked like hundreds more were filing into the street. Panic started to take over Jayde's mind.

There was nowhere to run, nowhere to hide, and the sleepers weren't stopping.

The laser blasts stopped abruptly. Jayde looked back and saw McCready's mech was being attacked. Three sleepers had grabbed onto the gun and jammed it. Jayde got back to her feet and started shooting at the sleepers on the mech, but her hand was shaking too much to get a straight shot off.

One of the survivors pointed behind her and shouted something, but Jayde couldn't make it out. She was so tired. Everything suddenly seemed to slow down, like she was moving in slow motion. She was aware of the sound of her own breathing. Her legs trembled with exhaustion. Her tongue had become sandpaper and brushed across her dry lips. The throbbing pain broke her from her reverie and she turned to the army of sleepers. If she was going to die here, she was going to die fighting.

Jayde blasted one sleeper in the skull, then another. The survivors joined her, fanning out on each of her sides. Wave after wave of laser blasts took down sleepers. The remnant of humanity fought with everything they had. A few of them were picked off by the undead, taken by surprise.

Ahead, the ranks of the sleepers grew fatter. Jayde tried not to let her fear take over again. It was a fight like nothing she'd ever experienced before. The sleepers stepped on their fallen comrades, some of them slipping in the blood and guts that drenched the street. It was a hellish landscape, something Jayde knew she would never be able to erase from her memory if she survived.

"Take cover!" It sounded like Stefan.

Jayde looked around, confused. Then she saw him. Stefan ran past them towards the army of undead, a grenade in each hand. Jayde looked for Anna but couldn't find her or Janice in the confusion. She turned back as Stefan launched himself into the midst of the sleepers. She couldn't see his face, but somehow, she knew he was smiling.

An explosion rocked the ground and shattered the windows of nearby buildings. The concussive force sent Jayde and the others stumbling backward. Jayde's ears were ringing. The explosion had cleared the street of the undead, but more of them were coming from behind.

"Forward! Hurry!"

Jayde didn't know if the others could hear her. She could barely hear herself. She ran forward, jumping over sleepers that hadn't fully been killed. Their twisted visages glared at her as their arms tried to claw at her legs. They cleared the nightmare and kept running, no order to their haphazard escape. Her hearing slowly returned, though there was a constant ring at the edge of every sound.

She looked over her shoulder and saw McCready had abandoned the mech. He jogged at the back of the group, stopping every few steps to turn and blast a sleeper with his Silver Flux rifle. They had gotten ahead of the sleepers, but their devastated ranks had quickly multiplied and an army of undead was on the heels of her group.

They still had a decent distance to travel, and Jayde wasn't sure she could make it. Every ounce of her strength was gone. She was drenched in sweat and her armor was holding it all in, making her skin sticky and slick. Her feet were killing her, and her knees continuously buckled, ready to give out at any moment.

Jayde gasped in deep breaths as she ran, the sting of cramps forcing her face to scrunch in agony. Her pace slowed from a run to a jog, and finally to a walk. She couldn't go any further. She stopped walking and bent over, her hands on her knees. Her pistol pressed against her kneecap, adding to the pain, but she didn't care. She was done.

She was giving up.

Some of the others continued past her, but a few stopped with her. She could hear them asking questions, but she ignored them. Her entire body was trembling now, and she stared at the ground, waiting for it to rush up and smack her in the face.

A strong arm lifted her up and she saw McCready's face. His expression was just as unreadable as always, but when his eyes looked into hers, she could see the worry in his gaze. She wanted to tell him she was fine and that she had everything under control, but she knew that was a lie.

"Come on, Captain," McCready said. "You've got a ship to reach and a crew to boss around."

Jayde could feel sweat rolling down her back and armpits and for some strange reason, that made her think of Gavin. She still blamed herself for his death and more often than not, she had nightmares of his death. If she gave up now, there would be no one would tell stories about him. Like the time he had almost kissed another man, having mistaken a person in drag as a woman. Granted, Gavin had been drunk, but it was still funny.

She laughed through the tears and held onto McCready's hand. They started walking again and Jayde could see the hill that led up to the *Determination* not far ahead. She didn't know why she had felt so hopeless all of a sudden, but she felt like a fool for even considering giving up. These people needed her.

Thunder rumbled overhead and Jayde looked up to see something flying toward their position. Her heart dropped into her stomach.

The Thraan were back.

5

THE VESSEL WAS COMING in low.

Too low.

Jayde and the others ducked as the ship flew overhead and crashed into the approaching sleepers. An explosion rocked the ground as the ship exploded, taking out at least a hundred of the undead.

"What the hell was that?" Jayde asked McCready. "Was that a Thraan ship?"

"No," the soldier answered. "It was a Convocation ship. I feel bad for whoever was in it. That was a terrible way to go."

"It bought us some time. Let's go."

"What's that?" McCready asked.

Jayde turned her gaze upward to where the soldier was looking. Someone was floating down in a parachute.

"I thought the Convocation pulled everyone to the front lines?" Jayde asked McCready over her shoulder.

"I think that's … Loch."

They both stared in stunned silence as the person glided lower and finally touched the ground.

It was Loch. He quickly unhooked himself from the parachute and lifted a rifle and blasted a sleeper.

"That was the craziest thing I've ever done!" Loch shouted. "I can't believe I'm not dead!"

"You will be if we don't get back to the ship!" Jayde yelled back.

The unexpected arrival of another person falling out of the sky bolstered the morale of the survivors and they quickened their pace. Jayde took the lead of the group again with the help of McCready. Loch jogged beside them, constantly glancing around nervously.

"What made you change your mind?" Jayde asked.

"The Convocation sent out a mass communication," he said. "The Thraan have begun their invasion. They've been destroying outposts left and right. The war for humanity has begun."

"It's always bad news," Jayde muttered.

"I thought it was important enough to warrant crash landing onto Earth," Loch said. "I still can't believe I did that." He walked backward and surveyed the group of survivors. "Where's Isa?" he asked.

"She didn't make it," Jayde replied.

Loch stopped walking. "She's dead?"

Jayde also stopped and placed a hand on his shoulder. "I'm sorry. She fell into a trap and there was nothing we could do. I tried everything I could, but … I'm sorry, Loch."

"When she first got on the ship with us, I thought she was a lunatic. I mean, who follows another person across the universe on a whim? But these last few days she showed me that she wasn't crazy." Loch shook his head in denial. "I should have been here. I never should have stayed behind."

"I'm sorry," Jayde repeated again, "but we need to keep moving. There will be time to grieve later."

Jayde had never seen Loch upset about a woman before. He normally didn't spend more than a day with the same one, so it was never a surprise to see him with a different woman. Isa's death was really affecting him, though. Jayde didn't know what to say or how to react to his sadness.

She continued walking and Loch fell into step beside her. When they reached the bottom of the hill that led to the *Determination,* the number of sleepers following them had doubled. Whereas the survivors needed water and breaks, the undead didn't stop for anything. Jayde knew the hardest part of this journey was about to happen.

"The hill is steeper than it looks. It's going to be a rough climb, but don't stop. Don't give up. I'm going to stay here with McCready, but Loch is going up the hill with you. He'll let you into the ship. We'll be right behind you. If you need help, ask someone around you. We can't stop for stragglers."

The people were exhausted and it showed on their faces, but they also had fire in their eyes. These people had gone through hell to get this far and Jayde refused to let them down. They were so close to safety.

"Let's give them a minute to start up the hill, then we get up there and never look back."

"I couldn't agree more," McCready said.

They turned to face the horde of sleepers and started blasting the nearest ones. Jayde tossed a couple of plasma grenades into their midst and laughed maniacally as the undead were blown to bits. She put all of her fear, loss, and anger into her attack, killing more sleepers than McCready. He eyed her fury with admiration, but Jayde's focus was solely on destroying the undead and she didn't notice his look.

All of the noise was drawing more of the sleepers from the surrounding area. Hundreds were joining the others in the uphill climb. Jayde tossed another grenade and blasted open the heads of two sleepers with direct headshots. Her cartridge charge was running low. She reached into her bag to grab another, but she was out. Only two grenades were left.

"I think it's time to go," she told McCready. "My pistol is almost depleted."

The soldier nodded and turned around, quickly heading up the hill. Jayde grabbed one of the grenades and lobbed it into the center of a large group of sleepers, then turned and ran. Her leg muscles immediately protested and she had to slow her pace to a walk. She continuously glanced over her shoulder to make sure none of the undead was getting too close.

Most of the survivors were almost to the top of the hill, but there were two that were struggling. They stopped mid-climb to rest and didn't resume their climb until Jayde and McCready were about to pass them. One of them slipped and twisted their ankle, then tumbled down the hill. Jayde attempted to turn around and help, but McCready grabbed her hand and pulled her along.

Jayde watched helplessly as the person rolled right into the ranks of sleepers. The merciless massacre of the person forced Jayde to avert her eyes and focus on the climb. She didn't want to fall and join that poor soul.

They topped the hill and Jayde breathed a sigh of relief. That relief didn't last long as she saw that more sleepers were coming toward the ship directly ahead. Loch was standing beside the doorway to the *Determination,* the survivors filing inside. She hurried past Isa's pale corpse and removed the last grenade from her bag.

"Get the ship ready to go!" Jayde shouted as she ran past Loch.

She ducked under the ship and came out of the other side. There were roughly fifty sleepers moving quickly toward the ship. Jayde pressed the button on the plasma grenade and hurled it as hard as she could. It smacked one of the sleepers in the face and hit the ground before exploding. Jayde turned and hurried back to the other side of the ship where McCready and Loch were waiting for her.

"I said get the ship ready," she growled.

"I couldn't leave you out here alone," Loch argued.

"McCready's here," she pointed. "Go!"

Loch staggered into the ship and disappeared. Jayde looked around the area, debating on whether to get in the ship or to take out more of the undead. The look on McCready's face told her it was time to get inside. She smiled at the soldier and went inside the ship. McCready followed her and shut the door behind them, sealing the airlock.

"I don't hear the engines running," Jayde complained. "What's taking him so long?"

McCready shrugged. "What do you want me to do?" he asked.

"Designate rooms to the survivors, but not on level two. We haven't cleaned it since the Erillian Prime Minister thing and I don't want any surprises."

"On it."

"McCready," she called out before the man got too far. He turned and waited for her to say something. "Thank you."

"For what?" he asked.

"Saving my life back there. I don't know what happened to me."

"You had a moment of weakness, nothing more. It happens to the best of us."

"It shouldn't happen to leaders," Jayde said.

"It especially happens to leaders," McCready replied. "But you're welcome."

McCready offered her a rare smile and then left to direct the survivors. Jayde still didn't hear the engines running and her patience was already running thin. She stalked through the hallways to the observation deck. Loch was frantically tapping the console screen.

"What's happening? Why aren't we in the air yet?"

"Something is wrong," Loch said. He leaned forward and peered at the screen closely. "The engines aren't starting for some reason."

Jayde groaned. "Is there anything you can do from here?"

"I'm trying some of my normal tricks now, but ..."

"But?"

Before Loch could answer, the deck doors opened and Janice hesitantly stepped across the threshold.

"I'm sorry," she said, bursting into tears. "Anna's sick. She's not moving and she won't wake up."

"Get us out of here," Jayde said to Loch, then went with Janice to the third floor of the ship. McCready was still assigning people to spaces as Janice led her to one of the rooms. Anna was on the bed, unmoving, and her flesh was pale.

"When did this happen?" Jayde asked.

"She seemed fine when we got to the ship, but I did notice her skin was getting lighter. I just thought it was fatigue."

Jayde walked over to the bed and inspected Anna's arms and legs. She didn't see any wounds, but the girl was grimy and covered in sweat and dirt. Jayde rolled the girl onto her stomach and then she saw it. A small bite mark on her shoulder. There wasn't much blood, so Jayde couldn't fault Janice for not noticing it.

"She's been bitten," Jayde confirmed.

"Oh God, no," Janice said, falling to her knees. "No, no, no."

"The good news is we have a cure onboard the *Titan*. The bad news is, we don't know how to use the machines to make more of it."

"I know how to use those machines," Janice said. "I'm a nurse."

"Good. Now our only problem is we need to get off this planet. Stay here with Anna and let me know if there's any change in her condition. I'm going to get us to the *Titan* as fast as possible, but if she turns before that happens …" Jayde let the words hang in the air.

"Please hurry," Janice said, ignoring the threat.

"We're working on it."

Jayde left the room and McCready joined her as she got on the elevator.

"Anna needs the cure," Jayde said quietly. The elevator began its upward ascent and McCready remained silent.

"I left it on the *Titan*."

"That's where we're headed," the soldier said. "She'll be fine."

"That's where we're headed if the engines will start. Loch said they're not firing up."

McCready grunted in response. Jayde bit her lower lip and sighed out of her nose. She wanted this whole nightmare to end, but based on the news Loch delivered about the Thraan invasion, it sounded like it was just beginning.

"At least we can say we've been to Earth now," McCready said. "That's one item off my bucket list, at least."

Jayde laughed a little and shrugged. "That's true. It's a complete disaster zone, but yes, we've seen Earth with our own eyes."

The elevator stopped at the main level and the doors opened. Jayde stepped out and went back to the observation deck, McCready following quietly behind her.

"We're screwed," Loch said as soon as she entered. "I've tried every trick I know, but the damned engines aren't coming on."

"We're not screwed," Jayde said, though she didn't believe that herself. "We just need to figure out how to get them running. I'll go down to the engine room and … figure something out."

"You're not a mechanic, Jayde. Our mechanic, the wonderful and amazing Klaus, is on the *Titan* with no way of getting down here. I took the only working ship."

As if things couldn't get worse, pounding erupted from the hull of the ship as sleepers began attacking the vessel. Jayde looked from Loch to McCready. She could feel herself slipping back into the darkness that made her almost give up earlier.

"We're screwed," she said. "We're stuck on Earth."

6

JAYDE STARED OUT AT the mass of undead that had gathered around the *Determination*.

There were hundreds of them now, and they were trying to claw their way inside the ship. Jayde was considering turning the IDS on, but it didn't seem likely that the sleepers would be able to breach the vessel. Besides that, the ship couldn't take off if the defense system was on and she was hoping every time she pressed the button on the console that the engines would magically turn on. And every time she pressed the button, she was equally disappointed that nothing happened.

Loch had gone down to where the survivors were resting to see if any of them had any experience with spaceship engines. Jayde didn't think their luck would turn around, but she allowed Loch to check anyway.

"Jayde," the pilot's voice crackled over the intercom.

"Yeah?" she responded.

"Good news. There's a gentleman down here who says he's an engineer. He's not a mechanic, but he might be able to help."

Jayde perked up. "That *is* good news, Loch. Take him to the engine bay and see if you two can figure out what's wrong. Let me know as soon as you've got something."

"Will do."

The speaker went silent and Jayde leaned back into the chair and stared up at the ceiling of the ship. Now that they were safe, her mind had time to wander. She considered what Loch had told her about the Convocation's message. The Thraan were invading. It seemed so unreal to her. How could one race hate another so much that they felt the need to exterminate them from the universe?

She obviously didn't know the answer, nor could she guess a reason for such hatred. Maybe the Thraan felt like they were neutralizing a possible threat? Once Earth had built the technology for deep space missions, humanity had colonized the universe quickly. Perhaps too quickly. Or had they gone too deep into space and angered the aliens?

Jayde's thoughts were interrupted by someone joining her on the observation deck. She twisted around in the chair to see who it was and frowned when she saw it was Janice. Had Anna turned already? Her heart skipped a beat at the thought.

"What is it?" Jayde asked.

"Are we about to leave? Anna is getting worse."

"We're working on it," Jayde replied. "There's a problem with the engines."

Janice walked to the window and gazed outside.

"We're safe in here," Jayde said, thinking she knew the woman's fear.

"I don't doubt that. It's just …" Janice trailed off, then sighed. "How could this happen?"

Jayde remained silent. She knew that anything she said wouldn't make anything different. Besides, Jayde had asked herself that question a dozen times already.

"I should get back to Anna," Janice said as she turned around. "I just wanted to know when we were getting away from this place."

"As soon as possible," Jayde said.

"Thank you. For coming to help us."

"I'm just doing what anyone else would do," Jayde replied.

Janice smiled, the sadness and weariness evident in her steps. The woman left the deck and Jayde looked back up at the ceiling. She felt bad for the woman, for all of the survivors. In the blink of an eye, they'd lost family and friends. Jayde's experience on Ochillon was similar, but there had been time to grieve before the world as she knew it had ended. These people barely had time to register what was happening before their nightmare began.

Jayde realized she must have dozed off because when she opened her eyes, it was almost dusk. She groaned as she stood and rubbed her neck. She'd fallen asleep in a weird position and had strained her muscles. She pressed the intercom.

"Loch, what's the status?"

She waited a long moment, but there was no response. Her heart started beating fast and she wondered if something had gone wrong. Jayde grabbed her pistol from the console and left the observation deck. She stepped lightly and gripped her gun firmly. The main level of the ship was quiet. She took the elevator down to the third floor where the survivors were camped and stuck her head out.

Everything seemed fine. There were groups of people talking quietly and she could hear people snoring. That eased her mind, but she took the elevator down to the engine bay anyway. The doors slid open and she stepped out, glancing around the room. She didn't see anyone.

"Loch?" she called out.

Something metal clanged on the floor and she lifted her pistol. It had come from behind the engines. Her heart was hammering in her chest now. It was probably nothing, but given everything that had happened, there was no guarantee of that. She kept the gun up as she walked quickly to the engines and paused at the corner of the giant casing that covered the engines.

One, two, three.

Jayde stepped around the corner and smacked Loch in the face with the tip of her gun. Loch cried out in surprise. Jayde's finger slipped off the trigger with ease and she lowered the gun.

"You scared the hell out of me," Loch complained.

"I called your name," Jayde said.

"Well, we're working over here so I didn't hear you."

"You, working? That's laughable."

Loch rolled his eyes at her and turned around, handing a tool to the other man Jayde hadn't noticed. He was about the same height as Loch, but he wore glasses and his hair was slicked sideways.

"I'm Jayde," she said. "Captain of the ship."

"I know," the man said, squinting and sticking his tongue out as he leaned closer to one of the engines. He used the tool Loch had given him to adjust something she couldn't see, frowned briefly, then removed the tool and nodded to himself.

"That should do it," he said. "I'm Spencer. Spencer Burke."

"Nice to meet you," Jayde replied. "Did you say the engine is fixed?"

"I wouldn't say fixed, but it's as good as I can get it. It should turn on now, but I can't say how long it will run. The other one should be run like normal, but this one took a beating. It seems like something struck it, but I'm not sure."

That made sense. Jayde's landing had been rough, and she assumed that must have caused the issue.

"As long as it will get us to the *Titan,* I'm not worried about the engine. My mechanic is at the station and can make the necessary repairs once we get there."

"Like I said, it will turn on, but I don't know what it's going to do after it powers up."

"We'll just have to wait and see," Jayde said. "I appreciate your help. We'd be stranded if it wasn't for you."

"I just want to get far away from here. A new life somewhere else, you know?"

Jayde didn't blame him. She looked at Loch.

"Let's see if we can get out of here, shall we?"

The three of them took the elevator up to the third level. Spencer got off and Jayde thanked him again, then she and Loch went to the main level.

"Have you seen McCready?" she asked.

"Yeah. After everyone got settled, he ate something and drank a bottle of vodka. He's probably passed out in his room."

Jayde wasn't surprised. McCready could sleep through any situation. If only she were so lucky. Loch was walking faster than her and he reached the observation deck first. He sat at the console and held his finger over the screen.

"Ready?" he asked.

"I was born ready," Jayde replied.

Loch pressed the button. There was a loud booming noise, then the familiar hum of the ship as the engines came on. Jayde breathed a sigh of relief and sank into the chair beside Loch.

"That's the best sound I've heard in a while," she said.

Loch smiled and began prepping for launch. Jayde used the intercom to let everyone know they were about to take off, then watched Loch as his hand whizzed across the console. Her stomach growled in hunger. She couldn't remember the last time she'd eaten anything, but that wasn't important right now.

"Here we go," Loch announced.

The *Determination* shuddered as it left the ground. Several sleepers clung to the ship as it ascended, but most of them fell off as the ship picked up speed. Loch expertly guided the vessel toward the opening in the containment shield and Jayde was glad to have him behind the console again. Her piloting skills were rusty and after their harrowing escape, she wasn't sure she could have navigated them to safety.

They climbed higher and higher, the land below shrinking until none of the details could be seen. The *Determination* broke above the clouds and continued toward the atmosphere. Jayde looked at the console screen and noted everything was reading normal.

"Our luck may have just changed," Jayde dared to say.

She immediately regretted it. A loud explosion rocked the ship and Jayde fell out of her chair, sprawling onto the deck floor. She staggered to her feet and held onto the chair for support. The ship's alarm started blaring and Loch was frantically trying to keep the ship under control.

"What happened?" she asked.

"One of the engines caught fire," he shouted to be heard over the alarm. "The temperature reading in the engine bay is off the charts!"

A fire. In the ship.

Jayde had the feeling she'd just cursed them all. *Just once,* she fumed. *Just once I wish things would go in our favor.*

"We need to put the fire out," she said, turning to do just that.

"You can't go down there," Loch said. "The heat alone will burn you before you even get close."

"Seal the room, then."

"I already tried to," Loch said. "The fire must've damaged the wiring or something. The doors won't close and the elevator is disabled."

They looked at one another, each trying to figure out what to do.

"Can the other engine get us past the atmosphere?"

Loch looked at the screen and shrugged. "I don't know. Maybe?"

"Punch it," Jayde said. "Push the engine as hard as you can. We have to get past the containment shield or …" She didn't finish the sentence. Loch knew what would happen if they couldn't get past the shield.

He forced the remaining engine to run at full capacity and watched as the temperature continued to rise in the engine bay. Jayde turned her gaze to the window and waited. *Please,* she begged silently. *If there's any god out there listening, please get us past the shield.*

The *Determination* was shaking violently as it struggled to continue its ascent. Jayde used one hand to hold onto the chair and placed the other on the console. She imaged the chaos on the third level and how the survivors were probably freaking out. The lights flickered overhead.

"Turn off the power to any non-necessary systems," Jayde ordered.

Loch did so and the deck grew dark. The only equipment that remained illuminated was the pilot console. She watched as fire erupted outside the ship as the *Determination* reached the atmosphere. Jayde could feel sweat rolling down her sides from her armpits, but she didn't know if it was from the warmth spreading through the ship with the air conditioning off or from her anxiety.

"We're close," Loch said excitedly.

"Come on, baby," Jayde said, patting the console. "You can make it."

"The engine is starting to fail," Loch warned, his demeanor changing.

"Come on," Jayde repeated, this time as a whisper.

The next minute felt like an eternity for Jayde, but then Loch said, "We're through!"

She could see the containment shield not far ahead and her hope was growing. The ship slipped through the opening in the shield with a scraping sound. The bottom of the ship was a little low, but they made it past without further damage.

"We did it!" Loch shouted in triumph.

And then the ship rocked with another explosion.

7

"THE OTHER ENGINE IS gone!" Loch cried.

The console went dark and the hum of the ship died. The *Determination* was proverbially dead in the water. Jayde felt along the console and grabbed the emergency flashlight. She turned it on and blinded Loch with it when she pointed it directly at his face.

"Watch it," he grumbled.

"We need to get in contact with Klaus somehow. The *Titan* should have a way of pulling us in, but he won't know to be looking for us."

"He should already know," Loch replied. "The ship set off the distress signal when the fire broke out."

Jayde was relieved to hear that. "Let's hope that he was aware of the signal, then. I'm going to go check on everyone."

"I'll stay here. I don't like the idea of fumbling around in the dark."

"Suit yourself," Jayde said.

She left the deck and headed for McCready's quarters. The flashlight gave the shadows an eerie quality and Jayde's mind played tricks on her. She thought she could see the shadows moving, but when she shined the light at the movement, there was nothing there.

McCready's door was ajar and she pushed it the rest of the way open and stepped inside. The soldier was lying on his bed, arms and legs akimbo. He was snoring loudly. Jayde marveled again at the man's ability to sleep through anything. She left his room and noticed the temperature was getting warmer.

Jayde reached the stairwell and began the trek down to the third level. With the power out, the stairs were the only other way down. Despite her exhaustion, the descent wasn't too arduous on her legs. The thought of going back up the stairs, however, made her groan. She paused outside the door of the third floor and listened. She could hear voices, but nothing was discernable. She opened the door slowly and it creaked loudly.

"Who's there?" someone asked.

"It's Jayde. Is everyone all right?"

"I think so," the same person answered. "We can't see anything."

Jayde navigated her way to one of the storage closets and found a few more flashlights. She distributed them among the people and then checked on Anna. The girl was still pale and her breathing was ragged, but she seemed to be holding on. Janice sat on the floor nearby, staring off blankly.

"We've made it past the containment shield, but now the ship's dead. Klaus is on the *Titan* and should be able to help us."

"Who's Klaus?" Janice asked.

"He's my mechanic. I'm hoping there's a way he can pull us into the space station somehow, but we don't have any way to communicate with him now that the ship is down. Our distress signal fired off before the explosion, so Klaus should be aware of our situation."

Janice remained silent for a moment, then said, "We're not going to make it in time, are we?"

"We're doing everything we can to make sure we do," Jayde replied. She looked at Anna and worried that Janice might be right. The girl looked terrible.

"Jayde!"

Jayde turned and saw Loch standing near the stairwell. Some of the other people had shined their lights on him.

"What is it?" she asked, stepping out of Anna's room. His tone was a mix of excitement and fear.

"You might want to come to the observation deck," he said.

Jayde turned to Janice and offered a hopeful smile, but the woman's spirits didn't seem lifted at all. She left them and joined Loch at the entrance to the stairs. They began the climb up to the main level.

"I think Klaus got our signal," Loch said. "A tractor beam has started pulling us toward the *Titan*. There's a problem, though."

"Of course there is. What's the problem?"

"The *Titan's* bay is huge, so it's possible we could crash once the beam lets us go. We have no power, so there's nothing we can do to steer us clear from hitting anything."

"At least we'll be on the *Titan* and off Earth," Jayde said, trying to see the bright side.

"Yeah, if we don't crash and die."

Jayde ignored his negative comment and focused on climbing the stairs. By the time they reached the main level, her legs felt like jelly. Her muscles burned painfully and it was all she could do to put one foot in front of the other.

She was walking sluggish and Loch slowed his pace to match hers. They made it to the observation deck and Jayde could see a faint light streaming from the *Titan*. Loch was right, it was pulling her ship toward the space station. The movement was almost unnoticeable, but as she continued to watch, their speed picked up.

"Do you think Klaus knows how to use that beam?" Jayde asked.

"If I had to take a guess? That would be a no."

Jayde had to agree. Klaus was a mechanic and had, as far as she knew, never piloted a vessel before. And on top of that, he'd never served with the Convocation, so it was highly likely that he had no idea how to operate anything on the *Titan*.

"Go warn the others to prepare for impact," Jayde said. She handed her flashlight to him.

"I just did enough exercise to last me the rest of my life," Loch complained. "Can I send McCready to do it?"

Jayde shrugged. "If you can wake him. Either way, someone needs to tell them. And quickly."

Loch heaved an exaggerated sigh. He offered his mock salute and left her alone on the deck. She walked to the window and watched the distance close between the two vessels. Things were probably about to get a little rough. A few minutes later, Loch stumbled onto the deck.

"I can't see a damn thing in this blasted ship!" he cursed.

"Let me guess. You got McCready to go down there?"

Loch chuckled. "I did. It took a minute to wake him, but once he was awake and stopped swinging his fists at me, I told him to get down below. He grumbled a bit, but …" Loch shrugged.

"We're picking up speed again," Jayde said. "At least, I think we are. It's difficult to tell." She turned to Loch. "Is it just me, or is it getting harder to breathe?"

"You know, I was thinking that I was just really out of shape. The fire is quickly depleting our oxygen levels."

Jayde groaned. Time was against them. "Is there any way we can manually seal the elevator, at least?"

"I don't think so."

The *Determination* jolted suddenly.

"What was that?" Loch asked, grabbing hold of a chair for support.

"We're moving faster. A *lot* faster."

Jayde ran away from the window and grabbed onto Loch's hand, dragging him with her. She left the observation deck and continued down the hall. McCready stepped out of the stairwell and saw them running past. Before Jayde could tell him to run, he joined their sprint.

The ship pitched to the side roughly and all three of them fell to the floor. Jayde tried to get up, but the ship was either spinning or rolling and she was thrown against the wall, getting crushed between Loch and McCready. The soldier wrapped her in his arms protectively as they went flying across the hall and smashed into the other wall. Jayde heard the big man grunt, but his grip on her didn't weaken.

They tumbled across the floor again, but this time McCready used their momentum to his advantage and "walked" up the wall. Jayde watched helplessly as Loch was tossed back and forth like a ragdoll. A loud screeching sound forced Jayde to close her eyes and cry out in anguish.

The ship rocked one last time and went still. McCready and Jayde were on the floor again. She lifted her head and looked for Loch, but she couldn't see him in the dark. McCready's flashlight had been broken in the tumult and the entire hall was pitch black.

"Are you all right?" she asked the soldier.

"I think I broke some ribs," McCready replied.

Jayde felt and heard him moving around and he gasped in a sharp breath. "Yeah, definitely a broken rib or two."

"Oh God," Jayde said.

"Don't worry, I've suffered worse."

Jayde felt some relief at that. "Loch? What about you?"

There was no reply. Jayde sat up and wiped something wet from her forehead. She didn't need light to know it was blood. They had all taken quite a beating. *At least we're safe. I think.*

"Loch?"

She stood up and was overcome with a strong wave of vertigo. Jayde held her hands out in front of her for balance and after a few seconds, the feeling passed.

"I'm blind," Jayde said. "Can you see anything?"

"No," McCready answered. "Hold on. What's this?"

"What's what?" Jayde asked.

A soft blue light illuminated the hallway. McCready held up a holoscreen.

"That's Loch's," Jayde said.

"I'm surprised it didn't break like the flashlight did. That was a rough landing."

McCready stood up and used the light of the holoscreen to look for Loch. The soldier held his arm gingerly on his injured side. Jayde joined McCready and they found Loch a few feet away in a crumpled ball. McCready knelt and looked him over, then looked at Jayde.

"He's unconscious, but seems fine aside from some cuts."

"Good. I'm going to check on the others. Keep an eye on him but see if you can confirm if we're drifting in space or if we made it onto the *Titan*."

"Will do. Do you need this?" McCready held the holoscreen out to her. She almost declined, but the thought of walking down flights of stairs in the dark wasn't very appealing. She took it and made her way slowly back up the hall to the stairwell. If her ship wasn't damaged before from the fire, it was certainly busted up now.

Jayde had to continuously pause every few steps as dizziness swept over her. She kept her free hand latched onto the railing in case she got weak and fell, but she managed to make it to the third level without incident. The door was open and she could hear people groaning. She lifted the holoscreen up high and looked upon a scene of chaos.

People were scattered all over the floor. Anything that hadn't been secured had been tossed around and Jayde could see the light gleaming on blood.

"Is anyone seriously injured?" she asked loudly.

"A few of us got tossed around pretty good, but I don't think anyone has life-threatening injuries," a man's voice answered.

"That's good to hear. What about the girl? Anna. Is she hurt?"

Someone stepped into the light of the holoscreen and Jayde recognized Janice's face.

"She doesn't have much fight left in her," the woman said. "If we don't hurry, she's going to turn. Please, we have to do something!"

"Will someone help her carry the girl? We need to get her to the main level of the ship and the stairs aren't an easy climb."

The man who had spoken earlier walked over to Janice. "I'll help," he said.

Jayde was getting lightheaded. She gripped the railing tightly and swayed on her feet. Again, the feeling passed. *I must've lost more blood than I thought.* She noticed a woman crawling on all fours toward the stairs. The woman's hair was matted with blood and some of it was dripping onto the floor. As she moved her hand forward, she slipped in the blood and fell face-first onto the floor.

"Don't move," Jayde told her. "I'm coming to help you."

Jayde started down the stairs. A blackness grew on the edges of her vision and the last thing she saw was the metal floor coming up to meet her.

8

WHEN JAYDE OPENED HER eyes, she was greeted by a pounding headache.

"There she is." The voice sounded like Klaus's, but he was on the *Titan.*

Wait … am I on the Titan?

Jayde tried to sit up but the room began to spin and she quickly gave up.

"Where am I?" she asked.

Someone appeared next to her and she looked to see who it was. Klaus's face smiled down at her. "You're on the *Titan,*" he said.

She tried to remember what happened, but her memory was fuzzy. She blinked lazily a few times.

"How?"

"I pulled the *Determination* onto the *Titan* with the tractor beam," Klaus answered.

That was faintly familiar to Jayde.

"It's a finicky piece of equipment, apparently. I couldn't figure out how to slow it down and before I knew it, the ship was flung into the hangar bay. The *Determination* is going to be out of commission for a while, but she'll be back to her old self again once I'm done with her."

We crashed? That's great.

The sleepiness she felt was starting to wane and she tried to sit up again. Klaus helped her and she glanced around the room. She was in the infirmary. A few of the beds were occupied by people with bandaged heads, the gauze dyed red with blood. She spotted Anna, too. The girl's skin color was almost back to normal.

"How long have I been out?" she asked.

"Two days."

"Two days?" Jayde repeated incredulously. "What did I miss?"

"Not much," Klaus said. "Everyone has been recovering from the crash. Nobody died, so that's good, but a few people had some head wounds. Janice said everyone should heal in time."

"Where is Janice?"

"She's in the lab. She found the Erillian cure and has been busy replicating it. It seems to work. The girl over there was close to turning, but after Janice injected the cure into her, she's almost back to normal."

"Finally, some good news," Jayde said. "I have so many more questions about the Thraan disease now that we've seen what it did to Earth. This cure working has answered one of them, at least."

Jayde slid off the bed and held onto Klaus as she gained her balance.

"Has there been any updates on the Thraan invasion?" she asked.

"None," Klaus answered. "If the aliens have invaded human territories, I'm sure the Convocation have their hands full."

"I'm sure they do," Jayde said. She took a few steps on her own and felt comfortable enough to not rely on Klaus. "Where's Loch and McCready?"

"Loch's over there," the mechanic pointed to one of the beds. "McCready's probably eating. He's an endless hole sometimes."

"Speaking of food, I'm starving," Jayde said. Her stomach growled as if on cue.

"Want me to walk with you?"

"No, I think I'm all right."

Jayde walked over to Loch's bed. He was awake. A bandage was wrapped around his right arm and he had a massive bump on the side of his head.

"How are you feeling?"

"I can't say that I've ever felt worse," he said with a grin. "What about you? You had me worried. They said you collapsed going down some stairs and smacked your face hard on the floor."

"I don't remember any of it," Jayde said. "Other than a headache, I don't feel too bad."

"I'm glad you're all right. Klaus said we're going to be stuck here on the *Titan* for a few weeks while he repairs the ship."

"He told me the same thing."

"I don't mind getting some rest, but what's next on the agenda?"

"I'm not sure yet," Jayde said. She hadn't given it much thought. "But we've got some time to figure it out."

"I've got an idea whenever you're ready to talk about it."

—

As the days passed and Jayde's wounds healed, she began to think about Loch's question. What *was* next for her and her crew? Her ultimate goal was to retire in style, but if the universe burned under the wrath of the Thraan, there would be nowhere to live out that dream.

"What are you eating?"

Loch's voice broke her reverie. She looked at him as he sat across from her. He had a plate full of steaming food, steak and potatoes and a pile of green stuff she didn't recognize. One of the survivors was a chef and had been cooking nonstop for everyone.

The survivors had all started to take on various duties on the station and the majority of them had decided to stay on the *Titan.* A few of them, Janice and Anna included, decided to make a new life somewhere else. Jayde agreed to take them wherever they wanted to go once Klaus completed the repairs on the *Determination.*

"I had the chicken," Jayde replied. "It was good."

Loch nodded and dug into his food, filling his mouth and making noises that made him sound like some kind of wild animal.

"Do you have to do that?" Jayde asked.

"Sorry," Loch replied between mouthfuls. "It just tastes so amazing. That guy can really cook."

"I know. So, what was this idea that you wanted to talk about?"

Loch held up a finger and closed his eyes, then made more noises. He finished eating and pushed his plate aside.

"All right," he cleared his throat. "I think we should go back down to Earth."

"You want to go back down there?" Jayde asked incredulously. "For what?"

"I know it sounds crazy, but hear me out. The Convocation abandoned the planet, right? There's a planet's worth of resources just sitting there for the taking. We could make a few trips down there, grab some stuff that fetches a high price, and sell it to outposts or planets."

"Are you serious? We barely escaped with our lives and you want to waltz back down there for some cash?"

"Jayde, I know you're scared to face it all again. So am I. I'm just saying, it's something worth considering. I've talked to a few of the survivors, and they are on board if you are."

"I don't know," Jayde said. "I'll need to think about it. The danger alone …"

"Has never stopped us before," Loch interrupted.

"True. This is different."

"How so?"

"It just is," Jayde said. "There's a lot that happened down there that you don't know about. Besides, what if something happens? Something worse than what we've already experienced."

"Like what?"

"Someone could die."

"I suppose that could happen," Loch said. "But we know what to expect and could be prepared."

Jayde considered the idea for a moment in silence, then shook her hand. "No. I'm not interested in endangering anyone for the sake of profit."

Loch's expression didn't change, so Jayde guessed he was either expecting her answer or wasn't as fully vested in the idea as he made himself sound.

"What if there were more survivors?" he asked.

"There aren't," Jayde replied. "Logan said the only people he'd heard from was Stefan and his group."

"Yes, but we also know that the containment shield was disrupting transmissions from Earth. What if there are more people who need help but Logan couldn't receive their signals? What if now that the shield is partially lowered, we hear from more people needing help?"

Jayde hadn't thought of that. If that was the case, should it change her answer? She leaned back in her chair and crossed her arms over her chest.

"We can't leave people helpless down there. If there are more people, we will help them."

"And collect some stuff while we're down there?" Loch asked.

"Yes. As long as you understand that the people come first."

"Agreed."

—

The days turned to weeks and Klaus finished repairing the *Determination.* A small group from the survivors volunteered to train how to properly shoot guns in the event that there turned out to be more people in need of help. McCready oversaw their training to ensure they knew what they were doing.

Jayde knew the chances of there being more survivors was slim, perhaps impossible. The planet was completely overrun with the undead. She was tired of being on the *Titan* and was itching to be on the move. The few survivors who were ready to leave the station and start a new life had begun to voice their frustration. Jayde knew it was time to leave Earth behind. She had basically made up her mind and was ready to break the news to Loch.

He'd be upset with her. She knew that without any doubt. She wanted to make money, but not at the risk of losing more people to the sleepers. Today was the day that she would tell Loch what she was going to do. If he wanted to go, and she hoped he did, great. If he wanted to stay on the *Titan,* she couldn't keep him from doing so. She was heading toward the hangar bay, silently working out the conversation in her head.

"Jayde," McCready was coming in her direction. He had a serious look on his face.

"What is it?" she asked, growing anxious.

"You're not going to believe this, but we're getting a distress signal from Earth."

Jayde stopped walking. Was this a sign that she wasn't supposed to leave the *Titan* yet? Once her surprise waned, she began walking again and McCready fell into step beside her.

"How many are there? And what part of Earth are they located at?"

"Don't know," the soldier grunted. "We haven't received an actual message, just a flashing beacon requesting immediate assistance. It's a completely different location than where we first landed. Loch's excited for obvious reasons."

"I bet," Jayde replied. "Is there any indication of how long the signal has been on?"

"I don't think so, but Loch could tell you for sure. He's been waiting for something to come across the system like a lost puppy."

Jayde reached the hangar bay and found Loch. He was directing the volunteers to load the *Determination* with supplies. Jayde watched and waited in silence. Once the others had left, Loch smiled at her.

"We've got a signal coming in," he said.

"So I heard. Did you do a scan of the area?"

"Yeah. The beacon is coming from the outskirts of a large city. It's about ten miles outside the city proper. Thermal scans show the movement of at least a dozen life forms. They appear to be human, but the scans are limited for some reason. I'm guessing it's because of the containment shield."

"What's the plan, then? You've been waiting impatiently for this moment, so I assume you've got it all worked out?"

"I do. The team is loading the ship now with everything we need. Since the city is close, I think we'll be able to find some decent treasures to sell."

"And what about the sleepers?" Jayde asked. She knew Loch had the last few weeks to fine tune everything, but she wanted to be sure he was fully prepared. His focus seemed to be more on the money they could make than the risks involved.

"Each member of the team has been trained and signed off by McCready. They all have armor and plenty of charged cartridges. They saw some ugly stuff before we rescued them, so they aren't blind to the risks."

Jayde nodded. It sounded like he had it all under control. "All right, Loch. You're calling the shots of this mission. I'm coming along as well, and if there's anything I don't like, I'm pulling the plug. Got it?"

"Absolutely," Loch said.

"Good. Who should we leave in charge of the *Titan* while we're gone?"

"Janice has really stepped up. She's a natural leader, so she has my vote."

Jayde didn't disagree. The woman was a nurse in her former life, and she was intelligent and focused. She saw the best in everyone and was the first to volunteer for anything that needed to be done.

"Let her know," Jayde said.

Loch went to find Janice and Jayde turned to the hangar bay doors. Earth was waiting there, the beauty of its blue and white surface a deceptive cover for what really awaited down there. Jayde took a deep breath and tried to prepare herself mentally.

It was time to descend back into hell.

9

THE *DETERMINATION* LANDED MUCH smoother on Earth under Loch's control, and Jayde had no worries about the ship being able to get back to the *Titan.*

True to her word, she let Loch lead the excursion. He had brought five of the survivors as part of the team, each one vetted by McCready. The soldier felt all five were skilled enough with a gun, which did offer some relief to Jayde's worry.

Jayde holstered her laser pistol and opted to bring a rifle as well. She loved her pistol, but the rifle was quickly becoming a favorite. She glanced around her personal quarters to make sure she wasn't forgetting anything, then left the ship and met Loch and his group at the doors of the cargo bay.

Loch's small group was comprised of four men and one woman, besides Jayde and McCready. The woman was roughly the same height as Jayde, with short brown hair and a perpetual frown on her face. Her name was Cynthia and she didn't talk much. The men were as dissimilar in appearance as four different alien races.

Tariq was a tall, skinny black man with tattoos along his arms. Rustin was a redhead and if Jayde didn't know any better, she would have guessed he hadn't seen sunlight in years. He kept close to a tan-skinned man they called Saul, but Jayde knew that wasn't his real name. Lin was the last of the group. He was shorter than the others and had the slanted eyes that made his race evident.

Jayde watched the tree line as Loch gave his group orders and told them their roles. She had an odd feeling about this mission. It wasn't necessarily a bad feeling, but it wasn't good, either. She gripped her rifle tightly and walked toward the edge of the clearing they had landed in. It was a large open field surrounded by a heavily wooded forest. The map readings showed they were hundreds of miles away from the first place they had landed.

"Do you see anything?" Loch asked, stepping beside her.

"No. Are we ready to move?"

"Yes. I've sent Lin ahead as a scout to make sure we don't run into any surprises. I want this to go as smoothly as possible."

"That makes two of us," Jayde said, turning to look at the ship. It was covered in scorch marks and desperately needed to be washed, but despite all that, Jayde thought it looked amazing.

"After this, I'm taking the people who want to leave the *Titan* wherever they want to go. I figure that way we can sell what we find. If we think there's money to be had, then we can come back and do it again. Assuming this first endeavor goes well."

Loch smiled at her and headed back toward the group. Jayde followed him, continuously glancing around. McCready was standing with the group, a bored look on his face.

"Lin, you all right out there?" Loch asked, putting a communicator close to his mouth. There was a bit of static, then Lin's voice came back.

"All good. There're some dead sleepers that seem fresh. The people out there must have come through not long ago."

"Sounds like it. Keep me updated if you find anything else."

"We should stay alert," Jayde said. "We're assuming these people want to be rescued, but who knows if that's the case."

"That's a good point," Loch said. "I hadn't thought about people wanting to be left alone. That wouldn't explain the distress signal, though."

Jayde had thought along that same line, but it was better to be safe. Loch informed the others and they began their trek through the woods, following the route that Lin had scouted. He'd left white X marks along some of the trees so that the others knew where to go.

They followed the trail deep into the forest. The canopy overhead was thick and blotted out most of the sunlight. The dimness of the forest creeped Jayde out. She thought she could see shadows moving at the edges of her vision, but every time she looked, there was nothing. The passage of time seemed to slow as well. After twenty minutes of walking through the thick undergrowth of the forest, the trees cleared and the group was greeted by a paved road.

The road was well worn and parts of it were in disrepair. Jayde looked around for any sign of Lin's direction, but there were no white X's that she could spot. Loch noticed the same thing and looked at Jayde.

"Call him," she said.

"Lin, we're having trouble finding your trail. We're on the road. Which way do we go?"

Jayde felt like the pause lasted an eternity, but finally, Lin answered. He spoke quietly like he didn't want to be heard.

"Sorry, the paint ran out. I went right and followed the road. It's clear for half a mile, but the road goes through a city. I think I found the people with the distress signal, but something's off about them."

"What do you mean?" Loch asked.

"They are wearing bathrobes."

Loch kept his gaze on Jayde and they both shrugged.

"Maybe that's all they have to wear," Loch said.

"I don't think so. They've got a woman tied up. She's pretty bad off, too. I'm not sure, but it looks like they are doing some sort of ritual or something.

It's really weird. Should I backtrack and meet up with you?"

"Yes," Jayde told Loch. "Tell him to come back. He can lead us to where these people are. If we can see what's going on, then we can decide on a course of action."

"I thought you said I was in charge?" Loch asked with a smirk.

"Sorry," Jayde replied. "It's a habit."

"I know. I agree, regardless." Loch told Lin to return to the group and they waited in place for him. Jayde took the opportunity to drink some water and rest her legs. The pavement was too hot to sit on, so she rested in the grassy ditch beside the road.

They didn't have to wait long for Lin to return. He came jogging along the street and when he stopped, sweat was dripping down his face.

"I tried to run the whole way, but I cramped up and had to jog."

"You didn't have to hurry," Loch said, tossing him a canteen of water.

Lin drank deeply and wiped his mouth with the back of his hand. "I think those people are going to kill that woman. I had to run."

"Why do you think they are going to kill her?" Jayde asked.

"I told you, there's something off about them. Even if they don't kill her, why tie her up?"

Jayde had the same suspicion as Lin. She couldn't explain why, but she felt an urgency to get to the woman. Jayde slipped the rifle strap over her shoulder.

"We need to go," she told Loch. "We'll follow you, Lin. I know you probably need a break, but I think we don't have much time."

"I can make it," Lin replied. He took another drink from the canteen and handed it back to Loch, then began jogging back the way he'd come. Jayde followed him, holding the butt end of the rifle with her right hand to keep the weapon from flinging around.

Jayde looked over her shoulder and saw the others were following. McCready was at the rear of the group, his Silver Flux rifle in his hands. How he was able to jog with it, Jayde didn't know. It was annoying enough for her having to hold the gun to keep it from smacking her in the back of the head.

They followed the road for a quarter of a mile before Jayde saw the city Lin had mentioned. It flowed across the landscape in every direction. Jayde thought they were headed to the city itself and was surprised at how quickly Lin had made it back to them. They had at least another mile to travel.

Lin slowed to a walk and finally stopped, placing his hands on his knees and breathing heavily.

"You all right?" Jayde asked, stopping beside him.

"Yeah," he huffed. "Can we wait for the others to catch up?"

Jayde wanted to hurry and get to the woman before something happened, but if the people Lin talked about were a threat, she would need the help of the group. Loch and the others reached them and they took a moment to catch their breath and hydrate.

"We're not going into the city," Lin said. He pointed to the left, where a small dirt road disappeared among trees. "They're outside of a barn down that way."

Before Jayde could rush them onward, Lin started down the dirt road. He didn't jog, but he kept his walk at a brisk pace. Jayde ended up having to run to catch up to him and the others quickly followed.

"I was hiding behind one of the buildings up here," Lin said. "I heard someone shouting, so I took cover to see what was happening. That's when I saw the woman tied up and on the ground in front of the barn."

"How many other people did you see?" Jayde asked.

"There were six, but it sounded like there might be more of them somewhere."

Jayde looked back at the others and counted. There were seven in Jayde's group. That gave them the advantage of one if there really were only six of the others. Lin slowed his pace and pushed Jayde to the right, off the dirt road. Ahead, she could see the barn and a small group of people gathered in a circle.

She counted five people in the circle, but she didn't see anyone else. There were several small sheds and buildings designed for animals and Lin led her behind one of the larger buildings. The rest of their group joined them.

"Someone give me a boost," McCready said, nodding at the roof of the building. Tariq clasped his hands together, creating a 'step' for the soldier. McCready quickly climbed onto the roof of the building and Jayde waited impatiently for his report. A moment later, McCready looked down at them.

"There's five in a circle with a woman on the ground between them. She's not moving. I saw another one of them go into the main house."

McCready climbed down from the roof, dropping a few feet and landing easily. "There's something else," he said as he brushed his hands off on his pants.

"What is it?" Jayde asked.

"Those people aren't wearing bathrobes. They're wearing shrouds."

"Is there some significance to that?" Loch asked.

"Yeah," McCready replied. "That means they're alien worshippers."

"Oh, so they are crazy people," Loch said.

"They might be crazy, but they are definitely dangerous. The sigil on their shrouds represents the Thraan."

"Wait," Jayde said. "You're telling me those people worship the Thraan?"

McCready nodded.

"Why?"

"Who knows?" McCready said. "Either way, this isn't going to be a walk in the park. What's really confusing to me is why they have a woman. She's obviously a sacrifice, but worshippers don't generally kill people. They offer up others as a sacrifice to their gods."

"I didn't see any Thraan ships on the radar before we came down here," Jayde said.

"I didn't, either," Loch agreed.

"Maybe there's a Thraan ship on Earth?" Cynthia chimed in. "A ship could have been shot down and then they got trapped here because of the containment shield."

"Good point," Jayde acknowledged. "That is a possibility I hadn't considered."

"This is over my head," Loch said. "You're back in charge, Captain."

Jayde rolled her eyes and pulled her rifle off her shoulder. "We need to know exactly what we're up against," she said. "Lin, can you sneak around to the main house and see how many are in there?"

Lin nodded.

"McCready, get back on the roof and play sniper. As soon as Lin gets us a count, we'll—"

Jayde was interrupted by a screeching noise, followed by a loud roar. Her heart skipped a beat and she hurried to the edge of the building and risked a look. The barn doors had been opened and Jayde's eyes widened at what was slowly stepping out of it.

"Thraan," Jayde whispered.

10

THE MASSIVE ALIEN TOWERED over the robed men. Its head swung side to side slowly, sniffing the air. Massive clawed hands dug into the ground on either side of the bound woman and the alien leaned over her.

"Mighty Thraan God!" one of the men shouted. "See our sacrifice and find pleasure in it!"

Jayde turned to the others. "They have a Thraan and it's about to eat that woman."

"On it," McCready grunted. He climbed back onto the roof.

"We need a new plan," Loch said.

Jayde knew Loch was right, but she didn't know what to do. The words of the Erillian from Hetania echoed in her mind. *You don't fight the Thraan. You run from them.* If they ran, the entire trip back down to Earth would be a waste. *And an innocent woman would be dead.*

"Sometimes the best plan is no plan," Jayde muttered. Loch gave her a look that said she was crazy, but Jayde didn't care what he thought. They had to do something, and quickly. "Let's rush them. We have the element of surprise and we can take out a few of them before they realize what's happening. Guns up. Let's go!"

Jayde didn't wait. She lifted her rifle and stepped out from behind the shed and took aim at the Thraan. She fired off a shot. The laser blast sped through the air faster than she could see and struck the alien in the chest. It roared in anger, but Jayde wasn't sure if it actually did any damage.

The ring of robed men turned to her and one of them shouted something. They ran toward her. Jayde aimed at the man in the lead and blasted his head open. The other four slowed their pace, but a fifth man came running from the main building and his presence gave the others courage.

Jayde took aim at the newcomer, recognizing he was the leader. As her finger pulled the trigger, something heavy struck her from the side and she fell to the ground, dust flying into her face and her shot missing its mark. She blinked rapidly, confused. Through hazy vision, she saw Tariq standing over her.

"What the hell are you doing?" Jayde demanded.

"Hail to the Thraan," Tariq said, lifting a pistol and pointing it at her head.

He's a traitor. The thought angered her, but it also scared her. She couldn't fathom anyone in their right mind worshipping an alien as a god. Tariq glared at her, insane rage twisting his face into something out of a nightmare. *I'm going to die,* Jayde thought, but she refused to close her eyes.

Loch suddenly appeared and slammed a fist into the side of Tariq's head. The dark-skinned man staggered from the blow and dropped his pistol. Loch shook his hand, cursing from the pain. Jayde pushed herself into a sitting position and watched as Loch and Tariq struggled with one another, tumbling to the ground and rolling around.

Jayde turned her attention to the approaching alien worshippers and saw that their attention had been diverted. McCready was blasting the Thraan from the roof of the shed and the robed men were ducking for cover. Jayde got to her feet and looked around. Rustin was on the ground, clutching a wound that Jayde knew was mortal. There was nothing she could do for him. She grabbed her rifle and waited until Loch had Tariq pinned down, then slammed the butt end of the gun into Tariq's head.

The man went still. Loch got up and grabbed Tariq's fallen pistol, then started shooting at the other robed men. He hit one in the arm but narrowly missed the leader. Jayde took aim with her rifle and tried again to take out the leader. She missed and the man sprinted back to the main building and disappeared inside. Jayde was tempted to follow him, but they had a much bigger problem.

McCready's shots were dead on, but the armored hide that covered the Thraan only had black spots where the laser blasts had struck. Jayde stared at the massive alien and wondered how they were going to be able to kill it.

Cynthia sprinted past Jayde and made it to the woman that was tied up. She struggled with the bonds and didn't realize that the Thraan had noticed her. Jayde cried out a warning, but it was too late. The Thraan swiped a massive arm and cut Cynthia down with its claws. Her body fell to the ground in multiple pieces.

A blast from McCready's rifle hit the Thraan directly in the face. The alien roared and charged the shed. The robed men scrambled to get out of its way and the Thraan crashed into the shed, destroying the building. Jayde didn't see McCready anywhere.

"We've got to kill that thing!" Loch shouted at her.

"I know!" Jayde's eyes roamed up the alien's back, looking for anything that could be a weak spot in its armored hide. She could now understand more fully the Erillian's warning to her. The Thraan was like a tank.

"If only there was a way to get under its hide," Jayde said. And then an idea struck her. She hadn't brought any plasma grenades, but McCready had. "Help me find McCready."

The two of them rushed to the debris of the shed, keeping an eye on the Thraan and a wide berth of the alien's claws as it sniffed through the mess. Jayde spotted the soldier under a section of the collapsed roof. She hurried to his side. He had some cuts and scrapes but otherwise seemed unhurt.

"Any broken bones?" Jayde asked.

"I don't think so," McCready replied.

"Good. Where's your grenade?"

McCready grunted and tried to move his arm, but it was pinned at his side by the debris.

"It's at my waist, but I can't reach it."

Jayde slipped her arm beneath the roofing and tried to feel around for the grenade. Her heart was racing in her chest. She kept her eyes on the Thraan as it drew closer. Loch was trying to get the alien's attention, but the Thraan's sole focus was on Jayde. Her searching became frantic and she finally felt the grenade. She jerked her arm free, cutting the top of her hand on the metal of the roof and pressed the button, activating the grenade.

The Thraan got closer and roared. It was the exact moment Jayde was waiting for. She hurled the grenade. It flew through the air and into the alien's gaping jaws, disappearing within. Jayde laid prostrate and prepared for the explosion.

A moment later, the ground shook as the grenade detonated. Jayde's ears were ringing from the sound. She looked up and saw that the Thraan had been blown to bits.

"We killed it," Jayde said to McCready.

"That's great. Can you help get me out from under this thing?" the soldier grunted.

"No, I thought I'd leave you under there for a while," Jayde said, cracking a smile. McCready stared at her, unimpressed.

Jayde laughed and stood up. The ringing in her ears was still there, but it was lessening. She waved Loch over. He'd had the same idea as Jayde and had thrown himself to the ground. He brushed his hands over his armor, dusting himself off.

Together, they were able to lift the section of the roof up enough for McCready to crawl out from under it. The three of them stood silent, surveying the area. Cynthia and Rustin were dead. The robed men were gone, and so was Tariq. The alien worshippers had escaped, but their prisoner was still bound and lying in front of the barn.

"One of you check the house for Lin," Jayde said. McCready headed toward the building and Loch followed Jayde over to the woman. The woman was covered in blood, but upon inspection, Jayde thought most of it was from Cynthia's horrid death. Loch helped Jayde unravel the ropes and they helped the woman to her feet. She was weak and scared, but Jayde offered some calming words and the woman seemed to calm down.

McCready exited the main house and shook his head as he neared. "Lin's dead," he announced.

Jayde exhaled slowly. They had brought five survivors and were going to return to the *Titan* with only one. This mission had been a failure in her mind. A bloody one.

"Are there any others with you?" Jayde asked the woman.

She shook her head weakly. "No," she rasped. "It's just me."

Jayde and Loch aided the woman on the walk back to the ship while McCready kept a guarded watch on their surroundings. They made it back to the *Determination* without issue and didn't see any signs of the Thraan worshippers. Jayde was glad they didn't have any trouble, but it also worried her. Where had they gone? Did they have access to a ship? Would they try to leave Earth now that their 'god' was dead?

While Loch prepared the ship for launch, Jayde helped the woman get cleaned up. She found out the woman's name was Colette and she had been part of a small group that had survived the Thraan attack, but the robed worshippers had slaughtered the others and taken her captive. Jayde listened patiently as the woman explained what she'd experienced in the last few days. At times, the woman would pause and stare off for a moment before continuing her story.

The ship rumbled when they were in the air and Jayde had to lean uncomfortably close to Colette to hear her. Once Colette was done relating everything, Jayde took her to the kitchen for some food and water. Colette ate vigorously as if she hadn't seen food in years, then she fell asleep with her head in her arms at one of the tables.

Jayde left her there to rest and joined Loch on the observation deck. They didn't speak, but Jayde knew that Loch was likely having the same thoughts she was. Earth was too dangerous to be their gold mine.

A flash of light caught her attention and Jayde rushed to the window. A small spacecraft shot past them and through the containment shield's opening, disappearing into the blackness of space.

"I think that was our friends that formerly owned a Thraan," Loch said, trying to be funny. Jayde didn't laugh. She stared ahead, waiting to see if they were coming back. After a few minutes, Jayde was confident the people had fled and weren't preparing an attack. She left the window and glanced at Loch briefly before leaving the deck and heading for her personal quarters.

Jayde had made up her mind. They would not go back down to Earth. She would take the survivors to the destinations they had picked, then she and her crew would go back to taking odd jobs until they found the one that would guarantee their stylish retirement. They would go back to their normal lives. At least, as normal as they could be given what they'd been through and what the unknown future held with humanity and the Thraan now at war.

As long as she had her ship and her crew, Jayde knew that regardless of what the future held, one thing was certain: she was at home and surrounded by family.

ABOUT THE AUTHOR

Richard Fierce is a fantasy and space opera author. He's been writing since childhood, but began publishing in 2007. Since then, he's written multiple novels and short stories.

In 2000, Richard won Poet of the Year for his poem *The Darkness*. He's also one of the creative brains behind the Allatoona Book Festival, a literary event in Acworth, Georgia.

A recovering retail worker, he now works in the tech industry when he's not busy writing.

He's married and has three step-daughters (pray for him), three dogs (huskies!), a cat, and two ferrets. He basically has a zoo.

His love affair with fantasy was born in high school when a friend's mother gave him a copy of *Dragons of Spring Dawning* by Margaret Weis and Tracy Hickman.